D1631031
this
World

# Out of this World

VARIOUS

*Illustrated by*
***James Mayhew***

a division of Hodder Headline

First published in paperback in Great Britain in 2000
by Hodder Children's Books

The Federation of Children's Book Groups and
Hodder Children's Books are grateful to the authors
and original publishers for permission to reproduce extracts
from their original stories in this collection.

10 9 8 7 6 5 4 3 2 1



A Catalogue record for this book is available from the British Library

Hardback ISBN 0 340 77409 6
Paperback ISBN 0 340 77410 X

Typeset by Avon Dataset Ltd, Bidford-on-Avon, Warks

Printed and bound in Great Britain by
Clays Ltd St Ives plc, Bungay, Suffolk

Hodder Children's Books
A Division of Hodder Headline
338 Euston Road
London NW1 3BH

# Contents

*From the Federation of Children's Book Groups*

The Federation of Children's Book Groups is a national, voluntary organisation which exists to bring children and books together for enjoyment in homes, schools, libraries, bookshops and at fun events. Each year we organise a conference, promote National Share A Story Month and administer The Children's Book Award

*Out of this World* is our theme for 2000 and we are delighted to have worked with Hodder Children's Books to produce this wonderful anthology, with its special, 'unworldly' theme. We hope the anthology will be used to introduce children to different writers, perhaps to stimulate discussion or creative writing, but above all we are certain it will be enjoyed.

The Federation gratefully acknowledges the support of all those who have helped with this project.

For further information about the Federation, please contact:

The National Secretary, 2, Bridge Wood View, Horsforth, Leeds, LS18 5PE

or take a look at our web site - www.fcbg.mcmail.com

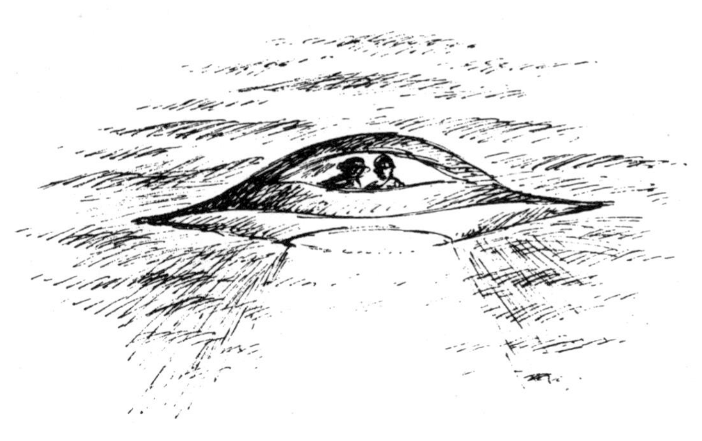

## AQUILA

*Andrew Norriss*

*When Tom and Geoff discover an ancient machine on a geography field-trip, they trigger a chain of strange and unlikely events. The machine has been buried for nearly 2000 years. When they sit in it the boys can make themselves invisible – and it will take them anywhere they want it to. But it's getting harder to keep Aquila a secret . . .*

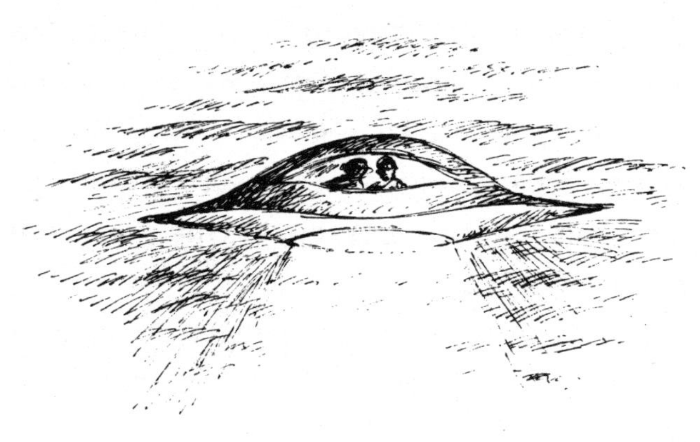

## *From* AQUILA

*Andrew Norriss*

The start of Miss Taylor's meeting was delayed for some minutes by the late arrival of Mr Hodge who had been at the hospital having his head X-rayed, but at a quarter past four it finally got under way.

'I'd like to thank you all for giving up your time at such short notice.' The Deputy Headmistress looked round at the dozen or so members of staff seated in her office. 'As you've possibly heard, I'm concerned about the activities of two boys - Tom Baxter and Geoff Reynolds - who were found this morning, in the library, trying to teach themselves Latin.'

A murmur of shock and concern ran round those of the staff who had not yet heard about this.

'In the last four days,' Miss Taylor continued, 'these same boys have approached Derek Bampford to ask about advanced power technologies. They asked Amy Poulson about the early navigation techniques used in the Flying Corps, and Peter Duncan found them on Monday trying to solve a maths problem in their free time . . . for fun.'

'They were at it again this morning,' Mr Duncan chipped in. 'Came to me at the end of the lesson. Wanting to work out something about a tap, a watering can and how big was the bath it filled in two hours.'

'Thank you, Peter.' It was the first Miss Taylor

had heard about that one. 'Now, that is exactly why we're here. I want to know what's going on, and the first thing we need to do is pool any information we have on their behaviour.' She looked around the room. 'Has anyone else noticed these boys doing anything odd in the last week or so?'

Eight people put their hands up.

At the controls of Aquila, Geoff banked to the right, and began a gentle descent that would carry them down towards Tom's garden. Both boys were filled with that deep satisfaction that comes from knowing that a difficult day has turned out rather better than either of them had dared to expect.

As Geoff said, once Tom had learnt to speak Latin, they would be able to ask Aquila so many things. They would be able to find out what the buttons did without the risks involved in just pushing them to see what happened. And when they knew what they did, they might even find out what some of them were for.

'Like that one,' said Tom, pointing to the button which had produced the blue light that had kidnapped Mrs Murphy's shopping trolley. 'I mean, what's it actually supposed to do?'

They were coming in over Mrs Murphy's garden as he said it and unfortunately Geoff chose exactly that moment to swing Aquila round towards Tom's garage.

The unexpected movement shifted Tom forward in his seat, and his finger made a momentary contact with the button at which he had been pointing. The contact lasted for only a fraction of a second before Tom snatched his hand away, but it was too late. The damage had already been done.

Aquila was now on full power, and the blue cord of light that appeared beneath it, instead of lazily snaking its way out, flashed to the ground like a bolt of lightning.

'What was that?' Tom asked, as Geoff took ˙ıs hands off the controls to stare at the ground ˀath them.

˙nk', said Geoff, 'that was Mrs Murphy.'

Mrs Murphy, in her garden, had been bending down to pick up one of her cats, when the bolt of blue light had engulfed her.

Neither she nor the cat had moved since.

Geoff landed Aquila by the burnt-out shed at the bottom of the old lady's garden, and the boys climbed out.

'Mrs Murphy?' Tom ran towards her. 'Mrs Murphy, are you all right?'

But Mrs Murphy did not reply. She still had not moved and, as Tom got closer, he realised she was not breathing.

Both she and the cat appeared to be completely frozen. Even her clothes and the cat's fur had a solid, unwavering look as if they'd been soaked in starch, and when Geoff stretched out a hand and tapped the old woman on the arm, it made a metallic ringing sound.

He opened his mouth to speak and then closed it again.

It was one of those times when it was difficult to know what to say.

'I've killed them, haven't I?' said Tom.

'Well . . .' Geoff looked closely at Mrs Murphy's face. 'I know she's not moving . . .'

'She's not breathing either.'

'No,' Geoff conceded, 'but if she was dead, wouldn't she have fallen down or something? I mean, she *looks* perfectly all right. Just . . . not moving.'

Tom's shoulders sagged. 'We'd better go and tell the police or someone.' He turned back to Aquila. 'My mother is not going to like this, you know. She is not going to like this at all . . .'

'Hang on.' Geoff caught his friend's arm. 'There is one thing we could try first . . .'

Miss Taylor had been taking notes. Most of the things people were saying she had already known, but some details were new, and had surprised even her.

Mr Urquart had given a list of the eight books e boys had taken out of the library in the last k, which included titles such as *A History* *ne* and *Great Palaces of Europe*.

Mr Rivers, head of the Science department, reported that they had also taken two books from his subject library - on lasers.

Mrs Ross, the English teacher, described how, after a lesson, the two boys said they had been reading H. G. Wells's *Invisible Man* and had quizzed her at some length on how invisibility might actually work. And the oddest revelation in some ways had come from Mr Weigart, in charge of Design Technology, who said that, the day before, he had found the two boys in his craft room trying to make a sextant.

Mr Duncan, when someone had explained to him what a sextant was, voiced the bemused astonishment of everyone there.

'What are they doing? What on earth is going on?'

'I think I may have the answer to that.' Miss Taylor stood up and started passing round a set of photocopies, neatly stapled together. 'If you'd all like to have a look at this? It's a copy of something we found in Tom's desk at lunchtime.'

Mr Bampford looked at the top page of his photocopy.

'Does anyone know what the Latin bit means?'

'It means "Any man can fly",' Mr Hodge spoke slowly and carefully, ' "if he rides on the back of an eagle." ' He looked across at the Deputy Headmistress. 'I'm surprised to find a child today knowing something like that.'

'You wait till you see the rest of it,' said Miss Taylor.

Doctor Warner was sitting in her tent when the phone rang. Deep in thought, the archaeologist was contemplating the object that had been dug up that morning from the earth directly beneath the body of the Roman centurion. It was, she knew, quite impossible. But impossible or not, it continued to sit where she had placed it, on the table in front of her.

It was a 100 per cent authentic, Red Indian ahawk.

noise of the phone slowly penetrated

her brain, and she picked it up.

'Yes, of course I remember you, Tom,' she said. 'What can I do for you?' She paused. 'You want the Latin for what?'

'Whatever you did to that woman, please could you undo it now,' repeated Tom.

There was a silence.

'Is that too difficult?'

'No. It's not difficult,' said Doctor Warner. 'I'm just wondering why anyone would want to say it.'

'We're sort of talking to someone,' Tom explained. 'Like on the Internet. But they only speak Latin. Please,' he added. 'You're the only person we can think of to ask.'

Doctor Warner stared at the ceiling of the tent for a few seconds. '*Quidquid illi mulieri fescisti, id facias infectum*,' she said eventually. 'Was there anything else?'

'Could you hang on a bit?'

In the background she could hear Tom repeating the sentence she had given him, and a moment later he was back on the line.

'It says "*Quae femina*?" What would that mean?'

'It means whoever you've got there wants to know which woman you're talking about,' said Doctor Warner. 'Are you boys in some sort of trouble?'

'No, no. No trouble. How can we say "The woman in the garden"?'

'I think before I do anything else,' said Doctor Warner, 'I really would like to know what's going on.'

'Could we explain some other time?' asked Tom. 'Only it's a bit urgent.'

'Who are you talking to? And why are they talking in Latin?'

'I don't know,' said Tom. 'They just are.'

'But they must know another language. Why don't you ask them to use it?'

'We can't,' said Tom. 'You see . . .' He broke off. 'How exactly would we do that?'

'What?'

w could we tell it to speak English, for ,' said Tom. 'In Latin.'

Doctor Warner sighed. 'Try "*Utere Brittanica lingua.*" '

'*Utere Brittanica lingua*,' Tom repeated, and Doctor Warner heard a sharp intake of breath, a whoop of triumph, and somewhere in the background there was Geoff's voice shouting, 'Fantastic! Oh, wow! That is unbelievable!'

'Tom? Tom, are you there? Is everything all right?'

'Couldn't be better, Doctor Warner.' Tom's voice had a quietly triumphant ring. 'And thank you. Thank you very much indeed.'

The phone went dead. On reflection, Doctor Warner decided it had been one of the oddest conversations she had ever had, and she wondered briefly if she should tell someone about it.

Instead, she put down the phone and picked up the tomahawk from the table. As she ran it through her fingers, all thoughts of anything else drifted out of her mind.

In her hands, she knew, she held the first

conclusive proof that, about a thousand years before Columbus, the Romans had discovered America.

All was quiet in the Deputy Headmistress's office, as the staff studied the photocopied pages Miss Taylor had given them, reading in an absorbed silence.

Mrs Ross was the first to speak. 'You're sure this is all genuine?' she asked. 'Tom Baxter wrote this himself?'

'Every word,' said Miss Taylor. 'I've seen the original.'

'It's unbelievable,' said Mr Duncan.

'I agree. It's quite unbelievable. But it's there.' Miss Taylor leant forward over her desk. 'Individually, I know, none of the things we've talking about mean anything very much, but taken together and particularly in the light of this –' she gestured to the copy of Tom's exercise book – 'I think there is only one conclusion we can come to.'

Around her, there was a slow, but distinct nodding of heads.

'The question is . . . what are we going to do about it?'

# KRINDLEKRAX

*Philip Ridley*

*Small, thin and weedy, Ruskin Splinter is the joke of his class at school. When he volunteers to play the 'hero' in the school play, no one really takes him seriously. But there is something lurking under the dark and cracked pavement in Ruskin's street. The mysterious Krindlekrax. Now Ruskin has a chance to prove how much of a hero he can be . . .*

## *From* KRINDLEKRAX
*Philip Ridley*

Ruskin lay in bed. Spread out across the blankets in front of him were Corky's walking stick, the tin helmet with the torch, and the pin from the medal. Tears dripped constantly from Ruskin's eyes and soaked the pillows and mattress.

Wendy came up to see Ruskin.

'Kiss,' she said.

'No,' Ruskin said.

'Tea?'

'No.'

'Toast?'

'No.'

'Baked beans on toast?'

'No.'

'Poached eggs on toast?'

'No.'

'Scrambled egg on toast?'

'No.'

'Fried egg on toast?'

'No.'

'Then what do you want?' Wendy asked.

'I want Corky back,' Ruskin replied.

Wendy sat beside Ruskin and stroked his forehead.

'He's not coming back, darling,' she said. 'You've got to understand that. He's dead. We've all got to die sometime. This is just the first time you've experienced it. Corky's body got tired, that's all.'

'No,' Ruskin said, 'Krindlekrax got him.'

'What's Krindlekrax?'

'The giant crocodile from the sewers. The one that Dad stole from the zoo. The one that cracks our pavement and scorches our bricks and digs up our roads. The one that's been searching for Corky for ten years. And now it's got him.'

Wendy shook her head and said, 'Oh, polly-wolly-doodle-all-the-day. Where do you get these stories from? You must get up. Everyone in Lizard Street is worried about you.'

'I don't want to see anyone,' Ruskin said. 'Everything that is me hurts: my toenails hurt, my hair hurts, my eyelashes hurt, my teeth hurt. I feel tired all the time and I can't stop crying. There's an ugly taste in my mouth that I can't get rid of and when I fall asleep I dream that Corky is alive and the ambulance was a mistake.'

'Have some tea,' Wendy said. 'Then you'll feel better. I've got some chocolate biscuits.'

But the thought of chocolate biscuits reminded Ruskin of Corky, so he started to cry again.

'Corky can't be gone,' Ruskin said, weeping. 'How can he be gone when he didn't finish his story?'

Later, Winston came up to see him.

'Want a cup of tea, yet?' asked Winston.

'No.'

'Toast?'

'No.'

'Baked beans on toast?'

'No.'

'Poached eggs on toast?'

'No.'

'Scrambled eggs on toast?'

'No.'

'Fried eggs on toast?'

'No.'

'Then what do you want?' Winston asked.

'I want Corky back,' Ruskin replied.

Winston left the bedroom and went downstairs.

Ruskin tried to sleep, but he kept on being woken up by the sound of Elvis's ball ' 'Da-boing!') and the squeaking of the pub sign

('Eeeek!') and the wobbling of the drain ('Ka-clunk!').

Lizard Street was continuing as normal.

But how could it? Ruskin thought. How could people continue as if nothing had happened? How could Mr Lace continue teaching and sucking his pencils? How could Mrs Walnut open her shop? How could Dr Flowers keep on being a doctor and sneezing? How could Mr Flick open the cinema and show *Henry V* on his new screen? How could Mr and Mrs Cave open the pub, serve drink, talk, smoke cigars? How could Elvis continue bouncing the ball, followed by Sparkey who continued to say 'Yes, sir'? How could his Mum, Wendy, continue making tea and toast? How could his Dad still look after fluffy animals and say, 'It's not my fault'? How could St George's School continue with its school play? How could everyone eat breakfast and dinner and watch television and go to bed and dream their dreams?

Ruskin imagined Corky's house, empty and

collecting dust; a packet of chocolate biscuits uneaten, the seats unsat, the lights unlit, the carpets untrod. All those little things that Corky had collected throughout his life, all the things he knew, the things he'd seen, the plays, the films, the books he'd read, everything was gone, invisible now, as if they had never been.

Ruskin started to weep again.

'I wish I could stop crying,' Ruskin said to himself, 'but I can't. It's as if my whole body is full of tears.'

The next day, Dr Flowers came to see Ruskin.

'TISHOO!' was the first thing Dr Flowers said. Then continued, 'Now what are you doing in bed? It's been a week now. Seven days is too long to . . . TISHOO! . . . stay between the sheets.'

Ruskin touched Corky's walking stick.

'I don't ever want to get up,' Ruskin said. 'I keep thinking of Corky and it upsets me too much to move.'

Tears trickled from Ruskin's eyes.

Dr Flowers gave him a handkerchief to dry his eyes. Then he stared at him from the end of the bed.

'But you can't stay in bed for ever,' Dr Flowers said. 'Everyone in . . . TISHOO! . . . Lizard Street misses you and . . .' His voice trailed away and he started to sniff.

Ruskin thought he was trying to ward off another sneeze, but - instead - Dr Flowers said, 'I can smell potatoes.'

And, sure enough, the next second Mrs Walnut came into Ruskin's bedroom, holding a packet of chocolate biscuits.

'These are for you,' she said, giving the biscuits to Ruskin.

'I can't look at biscuits without wanting to cry,' Ruskin said. 'They remind me of the way Corky used to lick the chocolate off them.'

'But they're a present,' Mrs Walnut said. 'You can't refuse my present. Corky wouldn't have wanted that.' Then Mrs Walnut started to sniff. 'I can smell cigar smoke,' she said.

And, sure enough, the next second Mr and

Mrs Cave came into Ruskin's bedroom, with a bottle of cherryade.

'This is for you,' said Mrs Cave, giving the bottle to Ruskin.

But Ruskin was still crying and wished they would all go away and leave him alone.

'My bedroom's getting too crowded,' he said. 'It's only meant for me. Not everyone in Lizard Street.'

But still more people visited with presents.

Mr Lace came with some coloured pencils.

Mr Flick came with a photograph of the actor playing Henry V.

They all stood at the end of Ruskin's bed and stared down at him. The room was so hot and stuffy with their breath that the windows started to mist up.

'Get out of bed,' said Mr Lace.

'We miss you in Lizard Street,' said Mrs Walnut.

'I miss your squeaky whisper of a voice,' said Mr Lace.

'I miss your knobbly knees,' said Mr Flick.

'We miss your fuzzy red hair,' said Mr Cave. 'Don't we, Mrs Cave?'

'Yes,' said Mrs Cave. 'We do, Mr Cave.'

And then, all together, they asked, 'Why don't you get up?'

'BECAUSE I MISS CORKY!' cried Ruskin.

They all looked at him in silence for a while.

'Does anyone remember that story about Corky?' Mr Lace said, looking round the room. 'About what he did when he was a child. Something about a medal.'

'Oh, yes,' said Mrs Walnut. 'It was before our time. Years ago, I think. Corky was a boy. He was playing on a dump . . . a dump at the end of the street. Where the pub is now.'

'That's right,' said Mr Cave. 'It was before the pub was built. There was nothing there but rubbish and rubble. Corky was playing on the site when suddenly he found something.'

Ruskin had stopped crying now. He sat up in bed and looked at Mr Cave.

'What did he find?' asked Ruskin.

'Something sticking out of the ground,' Mr

Cave replied. 'Pointed it was, and silver and very, very smooth. Made of metal.'

Ruskin leaned forward.

'Like a giant, silver fish head?' asked Ruskin.

Mrs Cave continued the story.

'That's right,' she said, puffing her cigar and flicking ash on to the end of the bed. 'It was something from the war and very dangerous.'

'A bomb?' Ruskin said.

'A bomb it was,' said Dr Flowers. 'Only Corky didn't know it was a . . . TISHOO! . . . bomb at the time, so he jumped on it and . . . TISHOO! . . . and it started ticking.'

Ruskin gasped.

'But that means,' Ruskin said, breathlessly, 'if Corky was to move the bomb would have exploded.'

'Precisely,' said Mr Flick, continuing the story. 'Luckily someone heard the ticking and yelled to Corky to keep still.'

'So Corky kept still?' Ruskin said.

'He kept very still,' said Mr Lace, sucking a pencil.

'He kept the stillest he'd ever been,' said Mrs Walnut, her potato smell getting stronger.

'He kept still for hours and hours,' said Dr Flowers, pinching his nose to ward off another sneeze.

'He kept still until some experts came and defused the bomb,' said Mr Cave, puffing his cigar. 'Didn't he, Mrs Cave?'

'He did, Mr Cave,' said Mrs Cave, puffing her cigar.

Ruskin was so engrossed with the story that he pushed the covers off him and stood up on his bed.

'So that's why he got a medal!' cried Ruskin, bouncing up and down on his mattress.

Later, after everyone had gone, Ruskin lay in bed and thought about the story.

Corky had saved Lizard Street. He had saved Lizard Street all by himself. He was a hero.

And now it was Ruskin's turn. Now he had to protect Lizard Street too. Protect it from the thing that cracked the pavement, scorched the brick-work and dug holes in the road.

Ruskin knew what he had to do. That night, while Lizard Street slept, he would tame Krindlekrax.

## HARRY POTTER AND THE PHILOSOPHER'S STONE

*J. K. Rowling*

*Harry Potter always thought he was just an ordinary boy. At least that is what his aunt and uncle always told him – in a nasty kind of way. But ordinary boys don't play games on broomsticks or meet dragons – and that's only the start of it. Harry Potter is just beginning his huge, magical adventure . . .*

## *From* HARRY POTTER AND THE PHILOSOPHER'S STONE

*J. K. Rowling*

Harry had never believed he would meet a boy he hated more than Dudley, but that was before he met Draco Malfoy. Still, first year Gryffindors only had Potions with the Slytherins, so they didn't have to put up with Malfoy much. Or at least, they didn't until they spotted a notice pinned up in the Gryffindor common-room which made them all groan. Flying lessons would be starting on Thursday – and Gryffindor and Slytherin would be learning together.

'Typical,' said Harry darkly. 'Just what I always wanted. To make a fool of myself on a broomstick in front of Malfoy.'

He had been looking forward to learning to fly more than anything else.

'You don't know you'll make a fool of yourself,' said Ron reasonably. 'Anyway, I know Malfoy's always going on about how good he is at Quidditch, but I bet that's all talk.'

Malfoy certainly did talk about flying a lot. He complained loudly about first years never getting on the house Quidditch teams and told long, boastful stories which always seemed to end with him narrowly escaping Muggles in helicopters. He wasn't the only one, though: the way Seamus Finnigan told it, he'd spent most of his childhood zooming around the countryside on his broomstick.

Even Ron would tell anyone who'd listen about the time he'd almost hit a hang-glider on Charlie's old broom. Everyone from wizarding families talked about Quidditch constantly. Ron had already had a big argument with Dean Thomas, who shared their dormitory, about football. Ron couldn't see what was exciting about a game with only one ball where no one was allowed to fly. Harry had caught Ron prodding Dean's poster of West Ham football team, trying to make the players move.

Neville had never been on a broomstick in his life, because his grandmother had never let him near one. Privately, Harry felt she'd had good reason, because Neville managed to have an extraordinary number of accidents even with both feet on the ground.

Hermione Granger was almost as nervous about flying as Neville was. This was something you couldn't learn by heart out of a book - not that she hadn't tried. At breakfast on Thursday she bored them all stupid with flying tips she'd got out of a library book called *Quidditch Through the Ages*. Neville was hanging on to her every word, desperate for anything that might help him hang on to his broomstick later, but everybody else was very pleased when Hermione's lecture was interrupted by the arrival of the post.

Harry hadn't had a single letter since Hagrid's note, something that Malfoy had been quick to notice, of course. Malfoy's eagle owl was always bringing him packages of sweets from home, which he opened gloatingly at the Slytherin table.

A barn owl brought Neville a small package from his grandmother. He opened it excitedly and showed them a glass ball the size of a large marble, which seemed to be full of white smoke.

'It's a Remembrall!' he explained. 'Gran knows I forget things - this tells you if there's something you've forgotten to do. Look, you hold it tight like this and if it turns red - oh . . .' His face fell, because the Remembrall had suddenly glowed scarlet, '. . . you've forgotten something . . .'

Neville was trying to remember what he'd forgotten when Draco Malfoy, who was passing the Gryffindor table, snatched the Remembrall out of his hand.

Harry and Ron jumped to their feet. They were half hoping for a reason to fight Malfoy, but Professor McGonagall, who would spot trouble quicker than any teacher in the school, was there in a flash.

'What's going on?'

'Malfoy's got my Remembrall, Professor.'

Scowling, Malfoy quickly dropped the Remembrall back on the table.

'Just looking,' he said, and he sloped away with Crabbe and Goyle behind him.

At three-thirty that afternoon, Harry, Ron and the other Gryffindors hurried down the front steps into the grounds for their first flying lesson. It was a clear, breezy day and the grass rippled under their feet as they marched down the sloping lawns towards a smooth lawn on the opposite side of the grounds to the forbidden forest, whose trees were swaying darkly in the distance.

The Slytherins were already there, and so were twenty broomsticks lying in neat lines on the ground. Harry had heard Fred and George Weasley complain about the school brooms, saying that some of them started to vibrate if you flew too high, or always flew slightly to the left.

Their teacher, Madam Hooch, arrived. She had short, grey hair and yellow eyes like a hawk.

'Well, what are you all waiting for?' she barked. 'Everyone stand by a broomstick. Come on, hurry up.'

Harry glanced down at his broom. It was old and some of the twigs stuck out at odd angles.

'Stick out your right hand over your broom,' called Madam Hooch at the front, 'and say "Up!" '

'UP!' everyone shouted.

Harry's broom jumped into his hand at once, but it was one of the few that did. Hermione Granger's had simply rolled over on the ground and Neville's hadn't moved at all. Perhaps brooms, like horses, could tell when you were afraid, thought Harry; there was a quaver in Neville's voice that said only too clearly that he wanted to keep his feet on the ground.

Madam Hooch then showed them how to mount their brooms without sliding off the end, and walked up and down the rows correcting their grips. Harry and Ron were delighted when she told Malfoy he'd been doing it wrong for years.

'Now, when I blow my whistle, you kick off from the ground, hard,' said Madam Hooch. 'Keep your brooms steady, rise a few feet and then come straight back down by leaning forwards slightly. On my whistle - three - two -'

But Neville, nervous and jumpy and frightened of being left on the ground, pushed off hard before the whistle had touched Madam Hooch's lips.

'Come back, boy!' she shouted, but Neville was rising straight up like a cork shot out of a bottle - twelve feet - twenty feet. Harry saw his scared white face look down at the ground falling away, saw him gasp, slip sideways off the broom and -

WHAM - a thud and a nasty crack and Neville lay face down on the grass in a heap. His broomstick was still rising higher and higher and started to drift lazily towards the forbidden forest and out of sight.

Madam Hooch was bending over Neville, her face as white as his.

'Broken wrist,' Harry heard her mutter. 'Come on, boy - it's all right, up you get.'

She turned to the rest of the class.

'None of you is to move while I take this boy to the hospital wing! You leave those brooms where they are or you'll be out of Hogwarts before you can say "Quidditch". Come on, dear.'

Neville, his face tear-streaked, clutching his wrist, hobbled off with Madam Hooch, who had her arm around him.

No sooner were they out of earshot than Malfoy burst into laughter.

'Did you see his face, the great lump?'

The other Slytherins joined in.

'Shut up, Malfoy,' snapped Parvati Patil.

'Ooh, sticking up for Longbottom?' said Pansy Parkinson, a hard-faced Slytherin girl, 'Never thought *you'd* like fat little cry babies, Parvati.'

'Look!' said Malfoy, darting forward and snatching something out of the grass, 'it's that stupid thing Longbottom's gran sent him.'

The Remembrall glittered in the sun as he held it up.

'Give that here, Malfoy,' said Harry quietly. Everyone stopped talking to watch.

Malfoy smiled nastily.

'I think I'll leave it somewhere for Longbottom to collect – how about – up a tree?'

'Give it *here*!' Harry yelled, but Malfoy had

leapt on to his broomstick and taken off. He hadn't been lying, he *could* fly well – hovering level with the topmost branches of an oak he called, 'Come and get it, Potter!'

Harry grabbed his broom.

'*No!*' shouted Hermione Granger. 'Madam Hooch told us not to move – you'll get us all into trouble.'

Harry ignored her. Blood was pounding in his ears. He mounted the broom and kicked hard against the ground and up, up he soared, air rushed through his hair and his robes whipped out behind him – and in a rush of fierce joy he realised he'd found something he could do without being taught – this was easy, this was *wonderful*. He pulled his broomstick up a little to take it even higher and heard screams and gasps of girls back on the ground and an admiring whoop from Ron.

He turned his broomstick sharply to face Malfoy in midair. Malfoy looked stunned.

'Give it here,' Harry called, 'or I'll knock you off that broom!'

'Oh, yeah?' said Malfoy, trying to sneer, but looking worried.

Harry knew, somehow, what to do. He leant forward and grasped the broom tightly in both hands and it shot towards Malfoy like a javelin. Malfoy only just got out of the way in time; Harry made a sharp about turn and held the broom steady. A few people below were clapping.

'No Crabbe and Goyle up here to save your neck, Malfoy,' Harry called.

The same thought seemed to have struck Malfoy.

'Catch it if you can, then!' he shouted, and he threw the glass ball high into the air and streaked back towards the ground.

Harry saw, as though in slow motion, the ball rise up in the air and then start to fall. He leant forward and pointed his broom handle down – next second he was gathering speed in a steep dive, racing the ball – wind whistled in his ears, mingled with the screams of people watching – he stretched out his hand – a foot from the ground he caught it, just in time to pull his broom straight, and he toppled gently on to the grass with the Remembrall clutched safely in his fist.

'HARRY POTTER!'

His heart sank faster than he'd just dived. Professor McGonagall was running towards them. He got to his feet, trembling.

'*Never* – in all my time at Hogwarts–'

Professor McGonagall was almost speechless with shock, and her glasses flashed furiously, '– how *dare* you – might have broken your neck–'

'It wasn't his fault, Professor–'

'Be quiet, Miss Patil–'

'But Malfoy–'

'That's *enough*, Mr Weasley. Potter, follow me, now.'

Harry caught sight of Malfoy, Crabbe and Goyle's triumphant faces as he left, walking numbly in Professor McGonagall's wake as she strode towards the castle. He was going to be expelled, he just knew it. He wanted to say something to defend himself, but there seemed to be something wrong with his voice. Professor McGonagall was sweeping along without even looking at him; he had to jog to keep up. Now he'd done it. He hadn't even lasted two weeks. He'd be packing his bags in ten minutes. What would the Dursleys say when he turned up on the doorstep?

Up the front steps, up the marble staircase inside, and still Professor McGonagall didn't say a word to him. She wrenched open doors and marched along corridors with Harry trotting miserably behind her. Maybe she was taking him to Dumbledore. He thought of Hagrid, expelled but allowed to stay on as gamekeeper. Perhaps he could be Hagrid's assistant. His stomach twisted as he imagined it, watching Ron and the others becoming wizards while he stumped around the grounds carrying Hagrid's bag.

Professor McGonagall stopped outside a classroom. She opened the door and poked her head inside.

'Excuse me, Professor Flitwick, could I borrow Wood for a moment?'

Wood? thought Harry, bewildered; was Wood a cane she was going to use on him?

But Wood turned out to be a person, a burly fifth year boy who came out of Flitwick's class looking confused.

'Follow me, you two,' said Professor McGonagall, and they marched on up the corridor, Wood looking curiously at Harry.

'In here.'

Professor McGonagall pointed them into a classroom which was empty except for Peeves, who was busy writing rude words on the blackboard.

'Out, Peeves!' she barked. Peeves threw the chalk into a bin, which clanged loudly, and he swooped out cursing. Professor McGonagall slammed the door behind him and turned to face the two boys.

'Potter, this is Oliver Wood. Wood – I've found you a Seeker.'

Wood's expression changed from puzzlement to delight.

'Are you serious, Professor?'

'Absolutely,' said Professor McGonagall crisply. 'The boy's a natural. I've never seen anything like it. Was that your first time on a broomstick, Potter?'

Harry nodded silently. He didn't have a clue what was going on, but he didn't seem to be being expelled, and some of the feeling started coming back to his legs.

'He caught that thing in his hand after a fifty-foot dive,' Professor McGonagall told Wood. 'Didn't even scratch himself. Charlie Weasley couldn't have done it.'

Wood was now looking as though all his dreams had come true at once.

'Ever seen a game of Quidditch, Potter?' he asked excitedly.

'Wood's captain of the Gryffindor team,' Professor McGonagall explained.

'He's just the build for a Seeker, too,' said Wood, now walking around Harry and staring at him. 'Light – speedy – we'll have to get him a decent broom, Professor – a Nimbus Two Thousand or a Cleansweep Seven, I'd say.'

'I shall speak to Professor Dumbledore and see if we can't bend the first year rule. Heaven knows, we need a better team than last year. *Flattened* in that last match by Slytherin, I couldn't look Severus Snape in the face for weeks . . .'

Professor McGonagall peered sternly over her glasses at Harry.

'I want to hear you're training hard, Potter, or I may change my mind about punishing you.'

'Your father would have been proud,' she said. 'He was an excellent Quidditch player himself.'

## MATILDA

*Roald Dahl*

*Matilda has a gloomy life. Her parents can't stand the sight of her, and most of the time she's ignored. But Matilda is an exceptional and gifted child – something she discovers when she starts at school. Bullied by her horrible headmistress, Matilda finds the power to fight back – in the best, most satisfying, and wonderful way . . .*

## *From* MATILDA
### *Roald Dahl*

Matilda sat down again at her desk. The Trunchbull seated herself behind the teacher's table. It was the first time she had sat down during the lesson. Then she reached out a hand and took hold of her water-jug. Still holding the jug by the handle but not lifting it yet, she said, 'I have never been able to understand why small children are so disgusting. They are the bane of my life. They are like insects. They should be got rid of as early as possible. We get rid of flies with fly-spray and by hanging up fly-paper. I have often thought of inventing a spray for getting rid of small children. How splendid it would be to walk into this classroom with a gigantic spray-gun in my hands and start pumping it. Or better still, some huge strips of sticky paper. I would hang them all round the school and you'd all get stuck to them and that would be the end of it. Wouldn't that be a good idea. Miss Honey?'

'If it's meant to be a joke, Headmistress, I don't think it's a very funny one,' Miss Honey said from the back of the class.

'You wouldn't, would you, Miss Honey,' the Trunchbull said. 'And it's *not* meant to be a joke. My idea of a perfect school, Miss Honey, is one that has no children in it at all. One of these days I shall start up a school like that. I think it will be very successful.'

The woman's mad, Miss Honey was telling

herself. She's round the twist. She's the one who ought to be got rid of.

The Trunchbull now lifted the large blue porcelain water-jug and poured some water into her glass. And suddenly, with the water, out came the long slimy newt straight into the glass, *plop*!

The Trunchbull let out a yell and leapt off her chair as though a firecracker had gone off underneath her. And now the children also saw the long thin slimy yellow-bellied lizard-like creature twisting and turning in the glass, and they squirmed and jumped about as well, shouting, 'What is it? Oh, it's disgusting! It's a snake! It's a baby crocodile! It's an alligator!'

'Look out, Miss Trunchbull!' cried Lavender. 'I'll bet it bites!'

The Trunchbull, this mighty female giant, stood there in her green breeches, quivering like a blancmange. She was especially furious that someone had succeeded in making her jump and yell like that because she prided herself on her toughness. She stared at the creature twisting and wriggling in the glass. Curiously enough, she had never seen a newt before. Natural history was not her strong point. She hadn't the faintest idea what this thing was. It certainly looked extremely unpleasant. Slowly she sat down again in her chair. She looked at this moment more terrifying than ever before. The fires of fury and hatred were smouldering in her small black eyes.

'Matilda!' she barked. 'Stand up!'

'Who, me?' Matilda said. 'What have *I* done?'

'Stand up, you disgusting little cockroach!'

'I haven't done anything, Miss Trunchbull, honestly I haven't. I've never seen that slimy thing before!'

'Stand up at once, you filthy little maggot!'

Reluctantly, Matilda got to her feet. She was in the second row. Lavender was in the row behind her, feeling a bit guilty. She hadn't intended to get her friend into trouble. On the other hand, she was certainly not about to own up.

'You are a vile, repulsive, repellent, malicious little brute!' the Trunchbull was shouting. 'You are not fit to be in this school! You ought to be behind bars, that's where you ought to be! I shall have you drummed out of this establishment in utter disgrace! I shall have the prefects chase you down the corridor and out of the front-door with hockey-sticks! I shall have the staff escort you home under armed guard! And then I shall make absolutely sure you are sent to a reformatory for delinquent girls for the minimum of forty years!'

The Trunchbull was in such a rage that her face had taken on a boiled colour and little flecks of froth were gathering at the corners of her mouth. But she was not the only one who was losing her cool. Matilda was also beginning to see red. She didn't in the least mind being accused of having done something she had actually done. She could see the justice of that. It was, however, a totally new experience for her to be accused of a crime that she definitely had not committed. She had

had absolutely nothing to do with that beastly creature in the glass. By golly, she thought, that rotten Trunchbull isn't going to pin this one on me!

'*I did not do it!*' she screamed.

'Oh yes, you did!' the Trunchbull roared back. 'Nobody else could have thought up a trick like that! Your father was right to warn me about you!' The woman seemed to have lost control of herself completely. She was ranting like a maniac. 'You are finished in this school, young lady!' she shouted. 'You are finished everywhere. I shall personally see to it that you are put away in a place where not even the crows can land their droppings on you! You will probably never see the light of day again!'

'*I'm telling you I did not do it!*' Matilda screamed. 'I've never even seen a creature like that in my life!'

'You have put a . . . a . . . a crocodile in my drinking water!' the Trunchbull yelled back. 'There is no worse crime in the world against a Headmistress! Now sit down and don't say a word! Go on, sit down at once!'

'*But I'm telling you . . .*' Matilda shouted, refusing to sit down.

'I am telling you to shut up!' the Trunchbull roared. 'If you don't shut up at once and sit down I shall remove my belt and let you have it with the end that has the buckle!'

Slowly Matilda sat down. Oh, the rottenness of it all! The unfairness! How dare they expel her for something she hadn't done!

Matilda felt herself getting angrier . . . and angrier . . . and angrier . . . so unbearably angry that something was bound to explode inside her very soon.

The newt was still squirming in the tall glass of water. It looked horribly uncomfortable. The glass was not big enough for it. Matilda glared at the Trunchbull. How she hated her. She glared at the glass with the newt in it. She longed to march up and grab the glass and tip the contents, newt and all, over the Trunchbull's head. She trembled to think what the Trunchbull would do to her if she did that.

The Trunchbull was sitting behind the teacher's table staring with a mixture of horror and fascination at the newt wriggling in the glass. Matilda's eyes were also riveted on the glass. And now, quite slowly, there began to creep over Matilda a most extraordinary and peculiar feeling. The feeling was mostly in the eyes. A kind of electricity seemed to be gathering inside them. A sense of power was brewing in those eyes of hers, a feeling of great strength was settling itself deep inside her eyes. But there was also another feeling which was something else altogether, and which she could not understand. It was like flashes of lightning. Little waves of lightning seemed to be flashing out of her eyes. Her eyeballs were beginning to get hot, as though vast energy was building up somewhere inside them. It was an amazing sensation. She kept her eyes steadily on the glass, and now the power was concentrating itself in one small part of each eye and growing stronger and stronger and it felt as though millions of tiny little invisible arms with hands on them were shooting out of her eyes towards the glass she was staring at.

'*Tip it!*' Matilda whispered. '*Tip it over!*'

She saw the glass wobble. It actually tilted backwards a fraction of an inch, then righted itself again. She kept pushing at it with all those millions of invisible little arms and hands that were reaching out from her eyes, feeling the power that was flashing straight from the two little black dots in the very centres of her eyeballs.

'*Tip it!*' Matilda whispered again. '*Tip it over!*'

Once more the glass wobbled. She pushed harder still, willing her eyes to shoot out more power. And then, very very slowly, so slowly she could hardly see it happening, the glass began to lean backwards, farther and farther and farther backwards until it was balancing on just one edge of its base. And there it teetered for a few seconds before finally toppling over and falling with a sharp tinkle on to the desk-top. The water in it and the squirming newt splashed out all over Miss Trunchbull's enormous bosom. The headmistress let out a yell that must have rattled every window-pane in the building and for the second time in the last five minutes she shot out of her chair like a rocket. The newt clutched desperately at the cotton smock where it covered the great chest and there it clung with its little claw-like feet. The Trunchbull looked down and saw it and she bellowed even louder and with a swipe of her hand she sent the creature flying across the class-room. It landed on the floor beside Lavender's desk and very quickly she ducked down and picked it up and put it into her pencil-box for another time. A newt, she decided, was a useful thing to have around.

## NIGHTMARE STAIRS

*Robert Swindells*

*Every night Kirsty has the same, frightening dream – someone is pushing her down the stairs. Kirsty tries to tell herself it is only a nightmare – but then she discovers a dark family secret, and a mystery that has never been solved. Until she gets to the bottom of it, Kirsty can never sleep peacefully at night . . .*

## *From* NIGHTMARE STAIRS

*Robert Swindells*

It must've hit you by now what's happened. What I'm saying. I'm saying Kirsty Miller's been here before. Have you never heard anybody say that about a new baby? Sometimes a baby'll get this look in its eyes - a deep, *knowing* look - and somebody'll say, 'Oooh, look at that - *she's* been here before.' Well, what I'm saying is, they're probably right without knowing it.

Oh, yes, I know it's far-fetched. I realise that. It was months before *I* could get my head round it but, you see, the evidence was all there. I knew the layout of the cottage at Nine Beeches, though I'd never been inside. I knew its loft used to be known as the Glory Hole. I knew Grandad Rodwell's first name - Bob - though nobody had ever used the name in my hearing. And I knew exactly what had happened to Grandma Elizabeth the night they bombed Viner's - I'd seen it, *felt* it, without ever leaving my seat in Mr Newell's class at Cutler's Hill Primary. And I was pretty sure I knew something else as well - something terrible, which nobody knew but me and a certain other person.

I struggled with all this stuff for months. Wrestled it in bed at night. I was desperate to tell someone but I didn't dare. Especially not the last bit - the awful suspicion I harboured about a member of my family. I was afraid that if I told anyone they'd think I was crazy and have me committed to one of those psychiatric hospitals they never let you out of. And I actually *felt* crazy. I wasn't sleeping. Couldn't concentrate at school. It felt like my life was crumbling. Falling apart. I had to *do* something.

One Saturday last autumn - it was the start of the October break - I was helping Mum with the vegetables. Dad was outside doing something to the car. I was at breaking point - really tensed up, and I said, 'Mum - how did Grandma Elizabeth die?' They'd never talked about it, see? Not in my hearing. All I knew was that she'd died a few months before I was born.

Mum gave me a funny look. 'What made you think about *that* all of a sudden, darling?' All of a sudden. That's a laugh for a start. I pulled a face. 'I think I know anyway, Mum. She fell downstairs, didn't she?'

'Who told you that, Kirsty?'

'Nobody. It happened at the cottage,

didn't it? At Nine Beeches?'

'*Somebody* must have told you, or you wouldn't know. *I* certainly never mentioned it. Was it Auntie Anne?'

I shook my head. 'I *told* you, Mum – it was nobody. I just – know, that's all. Why is it such a secret anyway? A lot of old people die falling downstairs.'

Mum nodded. 'I know, darling, but you see – there was your nightmare. Do you remember your nightmare? About falling? You used to get it almost every night. Your dad and I thought if you knew your grandma died from a fall it might make your nightmare worse. Sounds silly now but we did, and that's why we never mentioned it.'

I shook my head. 'I doubt if it'd have made any difference to my nightmare, Mum. Anyway you can tell me now, 'cause I know already.'

She shrugged. 'There's really nothing to tell, darling. Your grandma's legs were bad because of the war. She shouldn't have stayed on at the cottage after your grandad died but she wouldn't give it up. The staircase was steep and dark. One day she must have slipped or tripped or something, at the top. The postman found her next morning. He had a package for her, and when she didn't answer his knock he looked through the slot and there she was at the foot of the stairs. Her neck was broken. The doctor said she would have died instantly.'

She didn't, I thought. Not quite. There was no pain, but she felt everything going away.

'Poor Grandma,' I murmured, scraping diced carrots into the pan with the back of the knife. 'Dying alone like that.'

Alone my foot, I thought, lighting the gas. It was amazing how angry I felt.

Who was my anger directed at? Go on - have a guess. If you think it was directed at Auntie Anne, you're absolutely right. Well done.

I've told you a bit about my auntie. She's the one who'll hang on to a parking space for the pleasure of screwing up a total stranger. She's also the one in my dream who comes out of the spare bedroom and shoves me off the top step.

Oh yes. Of course I didn't realize till last summer. Or maybe I'd known all along but wouldn't let myself believe it. Because it is sort of unbelievable, isn't it? Her own *mother*, for goodness' sake.

In case you think I was jumping to conclusions – branding Auntie Anne a murderer on the strength of a dream and a coincidence – I'd better tell you something I forgot before. Remember I said we stopped once when I was seven to look at Grandma's old cottage? And Joe and I were fratching on the back seat while Mum and Dad chuntered on, and I heard Mum say, *There's something not quite right about that child*. Remember? Right. Well, Dad said something too. About the cottage. I didn't get it at the time, but I do now. By golly I do. This is what he said: *It's a pity your mother didn't get around to changing her will. If she had, we'd be living in the cottage and that ugly dormer would never have been built.*

Well. Doesn't take a university education, does it? To sort that one out, I mean. Those words of Dad's came back to me when Mum said Grandma ought not to have stayed on at the cottage. I didn't say anything. Not straight away. I went up to my room and had a think, and then I asked Mum another question, and her answer completed the jigsaw.

'Mum?' We'd eaten the meal. Mum and I were doing the dishes. Dad was in the front room, watching sport.

'Yes, dear?'

'What did Dad mean when he said it's a pity Grandma Elizabeth didn't change her will?'

She frowned. 'When did he say that, Kirsty? *I* don't remember.'

'Oh, it was years ago. In the car. What did he mean?'

Mum sighed. 'Well, I really don't understand why you're interested, dear, but if you must know it was like this. Your grandma's will left the cottage to Auntie Anne as the elder daughter, but when Grandma learned that Anne and Brian didn't intend having children, she decided to change her will so that I would get it. We had Joe, you see, and were trying for a girl. Unfortunately she didn't get around to it straightaway, and then she had her accident and that was that.'

Makes you think, doesn't it? Made *me* think.

## THE OWL TREE

*Jenny Nimmo*

*Joe and his sister are waiting for Mum's new baby to arrive. They've come to stay with their Granny Diamond – and it's here that Joe first senses the power of the spooky owl tree in the next-door garden. Granny loves the tree, but now her neighbour wants to cut it down. Can Joe, who is too scared even to climb the owl-tree, be the one to save it . . . ?*

## *From* THE OWL TREE

### *Jenny Nimmo*

'Gran!' Joe cried. 'Minna! Gran!'

They both came at once, colliding in the doorway, Gran out of breath and Minna frowning.

'There's a ghost outside!' Joe told them. 'Pale and horrible.'

Minna looked out. 'Well, it's gone now,' she said.

'Perhaps it was moonlight,' Granny Diamond suggested. 'Or leaves floating past.' She closed the window and drew the curtains.

'Whatever it was, it's outside now and you're in, Joe. So nothing can hurt you.'

'It screamed,' Joe whispered.

'You've got the wrong day, Joe. It's not Hallowe'en any more.' Minna sidled out with an unkind snigger.

Granny Diamond tucked Joe into bed and turned out the light. She left his door open so she could hear if he called her again. But she was walking so slowly Joe didn't think she would reach him in time to help.

In the room across the passage, Minna took a crumpled sheet of paper from under her pillow. She had written twelve names on the paper, girls' names in a neat column. She'd put them down for Joe but to Minna they were like the words of a bad spell. She wanted Mum to have another boy. If she didn't, Minna would have to be a tomboy for ever. And she was getting fed up with it. She wanted to be someone different, someone clever or musical like her friend Lucille. Secretly Minna longed to be an angel in the Christmas play, an angel like the one that hung over her bed. But who else would take on the job of family tomboy? Not Joe, who couldn't even climb a tree.

She pushed the list of names under her pillow and went to draw her curtains. But as she reached the window, something pale loomed out of the darkness. Minna saw the beat of angel's wings, heard a wild and chilling cry, and almost screamed herself. But flinging her hand across her mouth, she tumbled back on to the bed.

So there *was* a ghost out there! Joe's ghost.

Next morning they had an almost silent breakfast. Minna seemed to be weighed down with secret thoughts and Granny Diamond was stooped and sleepy. The fog outside was so thick they couldn't even see the wall, and the owl-tree had completely vanished.

Had the monster felled the tree in the night?

Was that why it had cried out? Joe didn't dare ask Granny Diamond, she wasn't herself at all.

As soon as breakfast was over he stole out of the back door and into the white mist beyond. Stepping carefully on to the path he began to make his way to the end of the garden. When he still couldn't see the tree or the wall, he stumbled forward, afraid of falling but desperate to see what lay behind the mist. He was almost there when a great branch loomed into view.

Joe heaved himself on to the wall and found that the branch came just above his waist. It would have been easy to swing himself over it, and to sit there bravely. But he wasn't quite ready for that. He just held tight to the branch and gazed at the top of the owl-tree. The fog had enclosed it in a cold blanket, but here inside, where the trunk wound up to the sky, it was warm and bright, and Joe could see hundreds of birds, some flickering between the leaves and others tapping at the trunk. A few sat very still regarding Joe with bright inquisitive eyes. What did they know?

From the top of the tree came a strange rustling murmur, 'Here . . . here . . . here . . .' The owl-tree had a secret, right at the top, and Joe would have to get it. But not yet.

When he got back to the house the kitchen seemed full of people. The Ludd twins were there with their mother. Minna was throwing things into a bag.

Mrs Ludd was surprised to see Joe. 'Oh,' she said. 'They didn't tell me about you. Are you Minna's brother? Or . . .'

Minna said, 'He's called Joe.'

'Minna's going to spend the day with us,' Mrs Ludd told Joe. 'Do you want to come?'

Minna and the twins weren't interested in his answer. They were chatting together in a corner. Joe shook his head.

Mrs Ludd smiled invitingly. 'Are you sure?'

'No, thanks,' Joe said. He had to think about the owl-tree, lay his plans.

Granny Diamond didn't see her visitors out. She stayed where she was, huddled in an easy chair. 'My bones are playing up today,' she said. 'What are you going to do?'

'Plenty,' Joe said.

The fog began to lift. Joe spent most of the day staring up into the owl-tree, counting the branches and trying to guess the distance between them.

Minna came back after tea. She couldn't stop talking about her wonderful day. When it grew dark Joe began to have second thoughts about his plan. But he heard Granny Diamond heave a sigh as she shuffled close to the stove, and he knew he would have to go through with it. She was fading before their eyes.

Minna's busy day had made her so tired she went to bed much earlier than usual. Joe followed, leaving Granny Diamond to read a paper by the fire. He didn't undress when he got to his room. He sat on his bed, waiting to put his plan into action. He chose the night for its darkness and secrecy. The monster wouldn't see him.

When the house was quiet, Joe crept downstairs. It was a cold, clear night and the sky was glittering with stars. But Joe didn't stop to look at them. He walked purposefully down to the owl-tree. This time, when he had pulled himself on to the wall, he swung one leg over the branch that leaned, so helpfully, within reach. Now that he was actually on the tree, with the rough bark under his hands and his feet swinging free, he found that he didn't dread the adventure ahead. The touch of the tree made everything possible.

Joe drew his feet on to the branch and crawled closer to the trunk.

The owl-tree shone pearl-grey in the night, its golden leaves turned to silver. Joe found a foothold and began to climb. The tree slipped branches under his feet and swept them close to his hands. Joe pulled himself up to the sky. Higher and higher. Now the houses were far below and he could see chinks of light from bedroom windows.

'I'm here,' Joe told the tree. 'So tell me how

to save you.' The tree whispered and sighed, 'Higher . . . Higher . . .' How high would he have to go before he had an answer? He put his ear against the trunk and heard a heartbeat deep inside.

'Tell me,' Joe begged.

There was a movement above him, the beginning of an answer. And then it came – a shriek and a wild, white thrashing over his head. And Joe, too frightened to cry out, was falling, falling, falling!

# PONGWIFFY AND THE HOLIDAY OF DOOM

*Kaye Umansky*

*Pongwiffy is depressed. So when a holiday brochure arrives in the post, she wastes no time in organising the trip of a lifetime. Armed with Hugo, her beloved hamster, Pongwiffy and all her friends (and their broomsticks) are off to the seaside – for a holiday none of them will ever forget . . .*

## *From* PONGWIFFY AND THE HOLIDAY OF DOOM

*Kaye Umansky*

'Well, this is nice, isn't it? Come on, Sharky, admit it's nice. Bowling along in a luxury air-conditioned motor coach on our way to the seaside. And all thanks to me,' said Pongwiffy, settling back in her seat with a pleased sigh. Up on her hat, Hugo (wearing a tiny pair of shorts and a jaunty straw hat) made himself comfortable and began to draw little Hamster faces on the dirty glass of the window.

'If this dirty old wreck is a luxury air-conditioned motor coach, I'm the sugar plum fairy,' grumbled Sharkadder, in a bad mood because Pongwiffy had pinched the window seat.

'Oh, don't be such an old fusspot. It's a nice little coach. Homely. I think it's quite clever, the way it's all held together with string. I loved it when the exhaust pipe fell off on the driver's foot when he was loading the Brooms into the boot. It's got character, this coach. It could have been a touch bigger, mind. We are a bit squashed.'

It would. They were. Fitting thirteen argumentative Witches and their assorted Familiars, Brooms and luggage into one saggy old fit-for-the-scrap-heap coach had been no easy task. However, after a good deal of squabbling everyone had finally managed to find a seat (except Gaga, who had elected to hang from the luggage rack with her Bats).

And now the holiday spirit was back with a vengeance as they trundled, creaking and backfiring, along the winding road that led away from dripping Witchway Wood towards the as yet unknown delights of the sunny seaside.

Everyone was really beginning to get the hang of things. There are certain traditional things you *do* on a coach, and the Witches were determined to get their money's worth. There were sweets to be passed and maps to be consulted. There was scenery to be admired. There were sandwiches to be eaten. There were passing wayfarers to make rude faces at. There were songs to be sung . . .

'Ten green lizards wiggling down the road,' started up the Witches in the back seat, led by Sourmuddle.

'Ten green lizards wiggling down the road. And if one green lizard should suddenly explode . . .'

'What a vulgar racket,' tutted Sharkadder, clutching her head. 'You'd think Sourmuddle would tell them, wouldn't you?'

'You would,' agreed Pongwiffy, looking around to see where Sourmuddle was. She located her slap in the middle of the back seat, about to commence a solo. 'On second thoughts, maybe you wouldn't. After all, it is a holiday. We're supposed to be letting our hair down.'

'Mine's down already,' said Sharkadder, taking out a mirror and examining her tortured curls with satisfaction. 'This is my holiday style. It's called Matted Mermaid. I think it rather suits me.'

In honour of the occasion, she had twined a bright green length of material printed with little anchors around her tall hat. Her hair was dyed to match and huge, unnerving octopus earrings dangled from her ears. A kind of Sea Theme, as she explained to anybody who would listen. The theme apparently extended to Dudley, who was kitted out with a matching scarf which he wore rakishly over one ear.

'Oh, it does. It's lovely. I must say you look

very stylish, Sharky. Very holidayish. I really like the Sea Theme.'

'Why, thank you, Pong.' Sharkadder brightened up a bit and fumbled in her handbag for her sea-green lipstick. 'I like to look my best. I don't like to let the Coven down. Not like *some* people.'

She stared pointedly at Pongwiffy's holey cardigan.

'Do you mind? These are my holiday rags,' said Pongwiffy, slightly hurt.

'What d'you mean? They're what you always wear.'

'No they're not.' Pongwiffy pointed proudly at some new red blobs. 'I've painted flowers on, see? Nice flowery print, very suitable for the seaside.'

Sharkadder opened her mouth to speak, then decided not to. Conversations about Pongwiffy's clothing never got anywhere. She knew. She'd tried.

'What's in the chest, then?' Pongwiffy pointed to the huge receptacle blocking

Sharkadder's bit of aisle.

'My make-up, if you must know,' Sharkadder said defensively. 'And Dudley's things. His cushion and his catnip mouse. And his fish heads.'

She smiled fondly down at Dead Eye Dudley, who was crouched on her lap, glaring up at Hugo with an expression of feline menace that would curdle cheese. Hugo was retaliating with a Hamster version which would strip paint.

'You should have been like me. Just brought the one bag,' said Pongwiffy, holding up a particularly tatty plastic one from Swallow and Riskitt that looked as though it had been used to strain curry.

'I wouldn't even put Dudley's fish heads in there,' said Sharkadder with scorn. 'Yuck.'

'Why can't you get fish heads in Sludgehaven-on-Sea?' Pongwiffy wanted to know. 'You're daft, you are. I'll bet you can buy any amount of fish heads there.'

'Not the sort he likes,' said Sharkadder firmly.

Just then, the coach went into a deep

pothole. Things came clattering down from the luggage racks. Everyone lurched and fell about. Greymatter made a mistake on her crossword puzzle. Macabre's bagpipes went off with a wild cry. Bonidle almost woke up. Sludgegooey dropped a bag of sherbet all over Ratsnappy and Gaga's bats flapped wildly.

'Bother!' said Sharkadder, who now had a trail of sea-green lipstick going up her nose. 'Now see!'

Ribald jeers and the jolly strains of 'For He's a Jolly Bad Driver' rose from the back seat. The driver (a bad-tempered Dwarf called George) tightened his grip on the wheel and did some terrible gear-clashing.

'Told you so!' grumbled Macabre from across the aisle. She was squashed uncomfortably between her bagpipes and Rory, and they really needed two whole seats to themselves. 'Gi' me a Broomstick any day!'

'When do we stop for lunch?' bawled Bendyshanks. 'Oi! Driver! When do we stop for lunch?'

'There's no stops,' said George firmly.

There was immediate consternation. No stops? All the way from Witchway Wood, over the Misty Mountains to Sludgehaven with *no stops*? After all those cups of bogwater?

'What d'you mean, no stops?' inquired Sourmuddle dangerously.

'Not on my schedule,' George informed her smugly. He wrenched the wheel, purposely swerving in order to drive through a big puddle, thereby spattering with mud a gaggle of rainsoaked Goblins who, for some strange reason, were trudging slowly in single file along the middle of the road.

'I don't do stops on this run.'

'Oh yes you do,' said Sourmuddle briskly, and twiddled her fingers. Much to everyone's delight, George's cap immediately rose from his head and sailed gaily out of the window.

Muttering under his breath, George slammed on the brakes and the coach juddered to a halt. To a chorus of loud jeers he dismounted and stumped back to pick up his cap from where it had landed – the large, muddy puddle he had just driven through. He bent down to retrieve it – then became aware that he was being watched by seven pairs of accusing eyes. They belonged to the rainsoaked Goblins he had just splashed with mud.

(Of course, they weren't just any old Goblins. Oh dear me no. They were Plugugly, Slopbucket, Hog, Eyesore, Stinkwart, Sproggit and Lardo, who were on their way to Gobboland with packs on their backs, sticks in their hands and a dream in their hearts.)

And now they had mud on their faces as well.

'I suppose you enjoyed dat,' said Plugugly. 'Splatterin' us wiv mud like dat. I suppose dat gave you a great big larf.'

'Yep,' said George. 'As a matter o' fact, it did.'

'Let's do 'im over, Plug,' urged young Sproggit, jumping up and down and waving his fists. 'Come on, come on, let's scrag 'im!

Let's roll 'im in the mud and throw 'is 'at in a bush!'

'Oh yeah?' said George smugly, jerking a thumb towards the coach, where the Witches had started up a hearty rendition of 'Why are We Waiting?'

'An' leave that lot without a driver? I don't fink so, some'ow.'

And with a confident air, he clapped his cap on his head and turned his back. The Goblins watched helplessly as he climbed in and the coach pulled away, belching exhaust fumes. The last thing they saw as it hurtled off around the corner was Agglebag and Bagaggle in the back seat, laughing merrily while making identical rude gestures.

''Ow come nuthin' ever goes right for us, Plug?' asked Lardo sadly when they had all finished choking.

'I dunno,' said Plugugly with a sigh. 'But it'll be all right when we get to Gobboworld,' he added more cheerfully. 'Come on, lads. We gotta long way ter go. Best foot backward.'

'There's somethin' wrong wiv that,' pondered Hog with a little frown. 'But I'm blowed if I can fink wot.'

And with great heavings and sighs and doleful head-shakings, the Goblins picked up their sticks and followed in Plugugly's wake.

## SKELLIG

*David Almond*

*Michael was looking forward to moving house, and to the arrival of his baby sister. But now the baby is critically ill and Michael's parents are convinced she won't survive. Michael feels useless and alone, until he steps into the crumbling old garage next door. From this point on his whole world changes – in the most miraculous way . . .*

## *From* SKELLIG
*David Almond*

The owls woke me. Or a call that was like that of the owls. I looked out into the night. The moon hung over the city, a great orange ball with the silhouettes of steeples and chimney stacks upon it. The sky was blue around it, deepening to blackness high above, where only the most brilliant stars shone. Down below, the wilderness was filled with the pitch black shadow of the garage and a wedge of cold silvery light.

I watched for the birds and saw nothing.

'Skellig,' I whispered. 'Skellig. Skellig.'

I cursed myself, because in order to go to him now I had to rely on Mina.

I lay in bed again. I moved between sleeping and waking. I dreamt that Skellig entered the hospital ward, that he lifted the baby from her glass case. He pulled the tubes and wires from her. She reached up and touched his pale, dry skin with her little fingers and she giggled. He took her away, flew with her in his arms through the darkest part of the sky. He landed with her in the wilderness and stood there calling to me.

'Michael! Michael!'

They stood there laughing. She bounced in his arms. They had lost all of their weaknesses and they were strong again.

'Michael!' he called, and his eyes were shining with joy. 'Michael! Michael! Michael!'

I woke up. I heard the owls again. I pulled

on some jeans and a pullover and tiptoed downstairs and out into the wilderness. Nothing there, of course, just the image of them burning in my mind. I stood listening to the city all around, its low, deep, endless roar. I went out through the shadows into the back lane. Though I knew it was useless, I began to walk towards Mina's boarded house. Something brushed against me as I walked.

'Whisper!' I whispered.

The cat went with me, slinking at my side.

The door into the garden was ajar. The moon had climbed. It hung directly over us. Behind the wall, the garden was flooded with its light. Mina was waiting. She sat on the step before the DANGER door, elbows resting on her knees, pale face resting on her hands. I hesitated and we watched each other.

'What took so long?' she said.

I looked at her.

'Thought I'd have to do this all alone,' she said.

'Thought that was what you wanted.'

The cat prowled to her side, brushed itself against her legs.

'Oh, Michael,' she said.

I didn't know what to do. I sat on the steps below her.

'We said stupid things,' she said. 'I said stupid things.'

I said nothing. An owl silently flew down into the garden and perched on the back wall.

Hoot, it went. Hoot hoot hoot.

'Don't be angry. Be my friend,' she whispered.

'I am your friend.'

'It's possible to hate your friend. You hated me today.'

'You hated me.'

The other owl descended and perched in silence beside its partner.

'I love the night,' said Mina. 'Anything seems possible at night when the rest of the world has gone to sleep.'

I looked up at her silvery face, her ink-black eyes. I knew that in a dream I would see her as the moon with Skellig flying silently across her.

I moved up to her side.

'I'll be your friend,' I whispered.

She smiled, and we sat there looking out at the moonlight. Soon the owls rose, and headed for the centre of the city. We lay back together against the DANGER door. I felt myself falling into sleep.

'Skellig!' I hissed. 'Skellig!'

We rubbed the sleep from our eyes.

Mina pushed the key into the lock.

We had no torch. The light that came through the chinks in the boards was pale and weak. We blundered through the dark. We held hands and stretched our free hands out in front of us. We walked into the wall. We caught our toes on loose floorboards. We stumbled as we climbed the stairs. We shuffled across the first landing. We felt for the handle of the door to the room where we thought we'd left Skellig. We inched the door open. We whispered,

'Skellig! Skellig!' No answer. We moved forward carefully, arms outstretched, feeling forward with our feet before we took each step. Our breath was fast, shallow, trembly. My heart was thundering. I opened my eyes wide, glared into the dark, seeking the shape of his body on the floor. Nothing there, just the blankets, the pillow, the plastic dish, the beer bottle rolling away from my stumbling feet.

'Where is he?' whispered Mina.

'Skellig,' we whispered. 'Skellig! Skellig!'

We turned back to the landing again, we stumbled up the next flight of stairs, we opened many doors, we stared past them into pitch black rooms, we whispered his name, we heard nothing but our own breath, our own uncertain feet, his name echoing back to us from bare floorboards and bare walls, we turned back to the landing again, we stumbled up the next flight of stairs.

We halted. We gripped each other's hand. We felt each other shuddering. Our heads were filled with the darkness of the house. Beside me was nothing but Mina's face, its silvery bloom.

'We must be more calm,' she whispered. 'We must listen, like we listened to the squeaking of the blackbird chicks.'

'Yes,' I said.

'Stand still. Do nothing. Listen to the deepest deepest places of the dark.'

We held hands and listened to the night. We heard the endless din of the city all around us, the creaking and cracking of the house, our own breath. As I listened deeper, I heard the breathing of the baby deep inside myself. I heard the far-off beating of her heart. I sighed, knowing that she was safe.

'You hear?' said Mina.

I listened, and it was as if she guided me to hear what she heard. It was like hearing the blackbird chicks cheeping in the nest. It came from above us, a far-off squeaking, whistling sound. Skellig's breathing.

'I hear it,' I whispered.

We climbed the final flight of stairs towards the final doorway. Gently, fearfully, we turned the handle and slowly pushed open the door.

Moonlight came through the arched window. Skellig sat before its frame, bowed forward. We saw the black silhouette of his pale face, of his bowed shoulders, of his wings folded upon his shoulders. At the base of his wings was the silhouette of his shredded shirt. He must have heard us as we stepped through the door, as we crouched together against the wall, but he didn't turn. We didn't speak. We didn't dare approach him. As we watched, an owl appeared, dropping on silent wings from the moonlit sky to the moonlit window. It perched on the frame. It bowed forward, opened its beak, laid something on the windowsill and flew out again. Skellig bent his head to where the bird had been. He pressed his lips to the windowsill. Then the owl, or the other owl, came again to the window, perched, opened its beak, flew off again. Skellig bent forward again. He chewed.

'They're feeding him,' whispered Mina.

And it was true. Each time the owls left, Skellig lifted what they had left him, he chewed and swallowed.

At last he turned to us. We saw nothing of his eyes, his pale cheeks; just his black silhouette against the glistening night. Mina and I held hands. Still we didn't dare go to him.

'Come to me,' he whispered.

We didn't move.

'Come to me.'

Mina tugged me, led me to him.

We met him in the middle of the room. He stood erect. He seemed stronger than he'd ever been. He took my hand and Mina's hand, and we stood there, the three of us, linked in the moonlight on the old bare floorboards. He squeezed my hand as if to reassure me. When he smiled at me I caught the stench of his breath, the stench of the things the owls had given him to eat. I gagged. His breath was the breath of an animal that lives on the meat of other living things: a dog, a fox, a blackbird, an owl. He squeezed me again and smiled again. He stepped sideways and we turned together, kept slowly turning, as if we were carefully, nervously beginning to dance. The moonlight shone on our faces in turn. Each face spun from shadow to light, from shadow to light, from shadow to light, and each time the faces of Mina and Skellig came into the light they were more silvery, more expressionless. Their eyes were darker, more empty, more penetrating. For a moment I wanted to pull away from them, to break the circle, but Skellig's hand tightened on mine.

'Don't stop, Michael,' he whispered.

His eyes and Mina's eyes stared far into me.

'No, Michael,' said Mina. 'Don't stop.'

I didn't stop. I found that I was smiling, that Skellig and Mina were smiling too. My heart raced and thundered and then it settled to a steady rolling rhythm. I felt Skellig's and Mina's hearts beating along with my own. I felt their breath in rhythm with mine. It was like we had moved into each other, as if we had become one thing. Our heads were dark, then were as huge and moonlit as the night. I couldn't feel the bare floorboards against my feet. All I knew were the hands in mine, the faces turning through the light and the dark, and for a moment I saw ghostly wings at Mina's back, I felt the feathers and delicate bones rising from my own shoulders, and I was lifted from the floor with Skellig and Mina. We turned circles together through the empty air of that empty room high in an old house in Crow Road.

Then it was over. I found myself crumpled on the floorboards alongside Mina. Skellig crouched beside us. He touched our heads.

'Go home now,' he squeaked.

'But how are you like this now?' I asked.

He pressed his finger to his lips.

'The owls and the angels,' he whispered.

He raised his finger when we began to speak again.

'Remember this night,' he whispered.

We tottered from the room. We descended the stairs. We went out through the DANGER door into the night. We hesitated for a moment.

'Did it happen to you as well?' I whispered.

'Yes. It happened to all of us.'

We laughed. I closed my eyes. I tried to feel again the feathers and bones of wings on my shoulders. I opened my eyes, tried to recall the ghostly wings rising at Mina's back.

'It will happen again,' said Mina. 'Won't it?'

'Yes.'

We hurried homeward. At the entrance to the back lane, we paused again to catch our breath. It was then that we heard Dad's voice, calling.

'Michael! Michael!'

As we stood there, we saw him come out from the wilderness into the lane. His voice was filled with fear.

'Michael! Oh, Michael!'

Then he saw us standing there, hand in hand.

'Michael! Oh, Michael!'

He ran and grabbed me in his arms.

'We were sleepwalking,' said Mina.

'Yes,' I said, as he held me tight to keep me safe. 'I didn't know what I was doing. I was dreaming. I was sleepwalking.'

## SNATCHERS

*Helen Cresswell*

*When Ellie Horner meets an angel called Plum in her local park, little does she know that he's her own, special, Guardian Angel, and he's here to protect her from the Land of the Starless Night. And when the wolf-woman comes to call, Ellie realises how much she needs Plum to take care of her on her journey into the unknown . . .*

## *From* SNATCHERS

*Helen Cresswell*

Mrs Horner was so pleased with her baby that she decided to have another. Not straight away, though.

'We'll wait until Ellie starts school,' she told her husband.

So they did. But you can't just order a baby like a bunch of flowers or a new carpet. By the time one did come along Ellie was already in the third class at school. This new baby was a boy called Sam and needless to say was the most beautiful baby there had ever been. Even Ellie thought so, at first. She would stare at him for hours on end and he'd stare back and say 'Coo! coo!' and curl his tiny fingers and toes.

But he grew up to be quite a terror, and by the time he was two would scream and stamp till his face was scarlet and tears gushed down his fat cheeks. Ellie honestly thought he might explode. She even wished he would sometimes. Mrs Horner didn't seem very worried about having a monster in the family.

'You were just the same at that age,' she told Ellie (who did not believe it, not likely).

Sam took so long coming that for seven years Ellie was an only child, and behaved like one. She read a lot of books and daydreamed and played secret games with imaginary friends. She had a whole world of her own inside her head.

It was one perfectly ordinary day in

September when it happened. Ellie had just bought a bag of plums. They were plump and golden and the juice dribbled down her chin. She sat on the wooden seat outside the library, and as she finished each plum she spat the stone to see how far it would go.

One or two people frowned at her, though she couldn't see why. She was spitting plum stones. Nothing the matter with that. With any luck, one day the library would stand in an orchard.

'Give us one!' said a voice.

Ellie turned and saw a boy of about her own age. He was rather raggedy, and had spiky hair and strange, liquid eyes.

'Who're you?' she demanded. 'Never seen you before.'

'Never mind,' he said. 'Give us a plum. Go on.'

'You don't go to my school.'

'Don't go to any school.'

'That's nice,' Ellie said. 'If it was true.'

'It is true,' the boy said.

'Must have a funny mum and dad, if they don't make you go to school.'

'Haven't got a mum and dad.'

'What? You must have.'

'Haven't.'

'Have.'

'Haven't.'

'Look,' Ellie said, 'everyone in the whole world's got a mum and dad. Don't you know anything? Don't you know how babies get born?'

She did. Your mum and dad made you, and you came out of your mother's belly button.

'P'raps you don't know who they are,' she said kindly. 'Are you an orphan?'

'No,' said the boy. 'If you must know, I'm an angel.'

'You must think I'm daft,' Ellie said. 'You're nothing like one. Where're your wings?'

'Lost 'em,' the boy said. He sounded sad, as if he really once *had* had wings, and had lost them.

'Mine are tucked flat under my sweater,' Ellie

told him. 'I don't use them a lot. And my spare pair's being washed.'

'Are you going to give me a plum or what?'

'OK.' She offered him the bag, and he took one.

To Ellie's surprise, he didn't eat it. He just squashed it between finger and thumb. From the pulpy mess he took out the stone.

'Funny way to eat a plum,' Ellie said.

He let the juicy flesh drop from his fingers, then licked them clean.

'Bet I can spit farther than you!' he said.

'Bet you can't!'

He spat. The stone flew from his mouth. It rose into the air in a smooth arc - and stayed there. Ellie stared. The stone hovered like a kestrel.

'I could make it go a hundred miles if I wanted,' the boy said.

'What's happening? Why doesn't it fall?'

She didn't like it. A plum stone was bobbing in midair in broad daylight outside the library.

'Make it fall!' she commanded.

'OK. Farther than any of yours though. Easy peasy.'

The stone started to fall, but not straight down. It sailed on and fell a good metre farther than Ellie's best spit so far.

'That'll be a tree one day,' he said smugly. 'A great big pink cherry!'

'Plum, you mean.'

He shrugged.

'What's the difference?'

'It's a plum stone. It's got to be a plum tree.'

'Look,' he said, 'I think you're forgetting. I'm an angel. Do anything, I can. If I want that plum stone to grow into a dirty great oak tree, it will.'

'And pigs might fly!' Ellie said.

'Bet you!' he said.

It seemed a safe enough bet. Even if he was right, oaks took years to grow. Hundreds of years.

'OK.' Ellie told him. 'Bet you . . . bet you . . .'

'Your bike!' the boy said.

'How d'you know I've got one?'

'Oh, I know,' he told her.

Ellie hesitated. She loved her bike. Besides, imagine the trouble she'd get into.

'What're you betting me?' she countered.

The angel (if that is what he was) looked at her thoughtfully.

'I bet you,' he said, 'a real pair of wings.'

'*What*?'

Ellie was all at once dizzy. She'd be able to fly like a bird – she'd always wanted to. It was what she pretended to be doing half the time when she was on her bike.

'Hang on,' she said. '*You* haven't got real wings, and you're supposed to be an angel. If you can just wish for them, why don't you get a pair of your own?'

'Don't know anything about angels, do you?' he said. 'The whole point of angels is that they do things for other people. Don't worry, I can get you wings, all right. P'raps not straightaway, though. You might have to wait a bit. Pity you can't get me some.'

He sounded sad again. Ellie was beginning to believe him.

'OK,' she said. 'Wings.'

'That I can't make that plum stone grow into an oak?'

She nodded. She knew he couldn't win. It would be years before the stone would be even a sapling.

He grinned.

'Here goes!'

They both looked over to where the stone had landed.

It happened so quickly that Ellie did not see the actual moment when the stone must have put out its first roots and started to grow. She only knew that it did, because there it was – first a sprout, then a sapling, then a tree. And one moment it was bare, then it had buds, then golden leaves. It was spinning through the seasons and Ellie's head went spinning with it.

The tree was already higher than the roof before she managed to croak a single word.

'Stop!'

Spring, summer, autumn, winter. Spring, summer, autumn, winter.

'Stop! Please! Oh stop!'

'I win?'

'You win.'

The tree stopped growing. It settled into the September day with a shiver of leaves already turning gold. It was an oak.

'Oh help! said Ellie faintly.

She was so shocked that she wondered if her hair had turned white. And what if – she looked down at her hands and saw with relief that they were still her own, and recognisable. If she too had gone spinning through the seasons, by now they would be wrinkled and spotted brown. By now she would be old. Ancient.

'Now what?' the boy asked. 'Want me to turn it back, or leave it?'

Ellie had not thought of that. She glanced round quickly. There were the usual Saturday-morning shoppers. Not one of them seemed to notice that an oak had sprung up, even though it was lit like a lamp in the sunlight on the dusty road. They would though, sooner or later, she thought. And Mrs Flynn in the library, she'd notice, bound to.

On the other hand, no one would know why. No one would connect it with her, Ellie Horner. Why should they? And the world needed more trees.

'Leave it,' she decided. 'Might as well.'

So he did. And in the end, of course, people did notice, and all kinds of questions were asked. Letters were written to *The Times* and clever men from universities came to look at the tree. But that was later, much later. What we want to know is what happened to Ellie next.

## SWITCHERS

*Kate Thompson*

*Tess is a Switcher. She can change shape to become another creature in the blink of an eye. Tess doesn't think anyone understands – until she meets Kevin, another Switcher. Now she no longer feels so different and alone. Together, Kevin and Tess discover how far their strange and special powers can take them, when they put their minds to it . . .*

## *From* SWITCHERS
### *Kate Thompson*

On that particular Saturday, her father had some work to do and told her that they would not be going into town before midday. Tess hid her delight. Now she would have the morning to herself. An unexpected bonus.

'All right if I go for a walk, then?' she said.

'Are you sure?' her mother asked. 'It's bitterly cold out.'

'I'll wrap up,' said Tess.

She put on jeans and her new puffa jacket, hat, scarf and gloves, and went outside. The wind wasn't strong, but it was colder, if anything, than the day before. Tiny particles of ice drifted in it, not quite snow yet, but a warning of it.

Tess looked up and down the road. During the summer holidays, there wasn't a parking space to be had for miles along the edge of the park, but today there were few cars. One or two stalwart owners were walking their dogs, and a few determined-looking families were playing soccer or frisbee, but mostly the park was deserted. In particular, to Tess's relief, there was no sign of Kevin. If he wasn't there today, the chances were that he hadn't been there on other Saturdays either. And if he hadn't, then he couldn't have followed her to the secret place she had found, and he couldn't have seen what she did there.

She began to relax a little as she walked across the bare fields of the park. She had always been careful, after all, very, very careful. It was vital that no one should see her and she had always made sure that they didn't. Kevin had just been bluffing. It was a clever bluff, too, because what teenager has not done something in their life that they would prefer their father not to know about? But a bluff was all it was, she was sure about that. If he tried again, she would invite him to come home with her and see what he had to say to her father. There was no way he would come.

She felt better, even light-hearted, as she came to the rough part of the park where her place was. Sometimes, when people were around, it was a little awkward getting in there without being seen, but today there was nobody within sight at all.

It was an area of small trees, ash and elder, with plenty of brambles and other scrubby undergrowth to provide cover. Tess looked around carefully. A woman had come into view, walking an Irish wolfhound which bounded with graceless pleasure across the open space of the park. Tess knew how it felt. She had tried a wolfhound once.

To be extra safe, Tess walked around her favourite copse and peered into one or two of the neighbouring ones as well. Well trodden paths ran between them all, and there was always a chance that somebody might be approaching, hidden by the trees. She stood still and listened for a long time. She knew the ways of the birds and small creatures well enough now to understand their voices and their movements. There was nothing to suggest that anyone apart from herself was making them uneasy.

She looked around one last time, then slipped into the copse. It was a place where she would not care to come alone at night. Even in broad daylight it was dark in there, and a little eerie. There were light paths through it that were clearly used quite often, and scattered here and there throughout the undergrowth were fast food wrappers and empty cans and bottles. Tess went on towards the middle, standing on brambles which crossed her path and ducking beneath low branches until she came to a place where the trees thinned a little. Here the undergrowth had grown up taller and thicker because of the extra light. A long time ago, a fairly large tree had fallen here, and the brambles had grown up around its remains. The smallest branches had rotted away, but the bigger ones were still intact and made a kind of frame.

Tess looked and listened one last time before she stooped and crawled into the narrow passage which led into the dark interior. Once inside, she was completely hidden from human eyes by the dense growth of brambles which covered the carcass of the tree. When she came out, she was a squirrel, full of squirrel quickness and squirrel nervousness, darting and stopping, listening, darting again, jumping.

Everything and anything in life was bearable as long as she had this. What did it matter if she had to wear that absurd uniform and go to that snooty school? At the weekends she could be squirrel, or cat, or rabbit, or lolloping wolfhound or busy, rat-hunting terrier. What did it matter if that vain and hungry boy was pestering her, trying to scare her? What did he know of the freedom of the swift or the swallow? What did he know of the neat precision of the city pigeon, or the tidiness of the robin or the wren? She would call his bluff and let him bully someone else. But just now, she would forget him as she forgot everything when she was squirrel, because squirrel hours are long and busy and full of forgetfulness.

The sun poked through the branches above, and if it wasn't the warm, autumn sun it might have been, it still didn't matter so much. Its bright beams added to the dizzying elation of scrurrying about and jumping from branch to branch, and Tess was too busy to be cold.

Squirrels do as squirrels must. It didn't matter that she would not be there to hibernate during the winter. Autumn was collecting time, so collect is what she did. But because she wouldn't have to eat her store of foodstuffs in the winter, it didn't particularly matter what she collected. Some things, like rose hip seeds and hazel nuts, seemed urgent, and could not be resisted. She stuffed the pouches of her cheeks and brought them to her den. Other things, like sycamore wings and the mean, sour little blackberries that the cold, dry autumn had produced, were less urgent, but she brought them anyway because they looked nice, and there wasn't anything else in particular to be done. If the other squirrels found her habits strange, they were too busy with their own gathering to give her their attention. The only time they bothered about her was when she ventured too far into someone else's territory, and then a good scolding was enough to put her right.

She knew most of the other squirrels. Earlier in the year, before school started, she had often spent time playing with them, engaging in terrific races and tests of acrobatic skill. She always lost, through lack of coordination or lack of nerve, but it didn't matter. It was sheer exhilaration to move so fast, faster than her human mind could follow, and to make decisions in midair, using reflex instead of thought. She remembered some of those breathtaking moments as she encountered particular squirrels, but there was no time for that kind of thing now. Life was rich with a different kind of urgency. Food was going to be scarce this year.

There was a clatter of wings in the treetops. For an instant the thicket froze like a photograph, and then its movement began again. Nothing more than a grey pigeon making a rather clumsy landing. Tess caught a brief glimpse of something shining on the ground and swooped down a tree trunk head first to investigate. At first she thought it was a ring pull from a drinks can, but as she got closer she saw that it was a real ring, a broad band of silver, scarcely tarnished at all. The metal grated unpleasantly against her little teeth, but she was determined to have it. She took a firm grip on it and pulled, but it would not come. A sharp blade of tough grass had grown up through it and become entwined with other grasses on the other side. She tugged again, and all at once was aware of another of those sudden woodland silences which always spell a warning.

She froze. She could see no enemy, but she smelt him, and he was close, very close. It was a smell she had never encountered before. She looked around carefully, and found herself face to face with the strangest squirrel she had ever seen. He was small and strong, his ears were sharp and pointed, and he was red, with black and white stripes running down his back. Every other squirrel in the copse was still, looking down at this oddity.

'He's not a squirrel at all,' thought Tess. 'He's a chipmunk. What on earth is a chipmunk doing in the Phoenix Park?'

As quick as any squirrel, the chipmunk darted forward and took hold of the ring in his teeth. As though reassured by this, the other squirrels relaxed and went back about their business. But Tess was infuriated. Whatever he was, wherever he came from, he was not going to have her ring.

She sprang forward and took a grip on the ring beside him. It may have seemed like a courageous thing for her to do, to take on this intruder, but she was supported by the knowledge that if she were in real danger all she had to do was to change back into Tess. Not only would she escape, but she would give her enemy the fright of his life.

Only once, so far, had she needed to do it, and that was when she had been a rabbit at dusk, not far from their last house. A fox had appeared from nowhere, and she had fled with the other rabbits towards their burrows. But the chap in front of her had been slow to get in, and the fox had been just about to close his teeth on her thigh. Instead, he was brought up short by a human leg, and he ran away home extremely frightened and bewildered.

She had been lucky. There had been no one around to see it happen. It was a last resort, but here in the darkness of the thicket she was prepared to use it if she had to.

But she didn't. As soon as she took hold of the ring, the chipmunk released it and used its teeth instead to cut through the tough grass. The ring came free, and Tess raced off along the thicket floor, holding her head high so that the ring would not get snagged on plants or fallen twigs. The chipmunk followed. At the door to her den, Tess dropped the ring and scolded him soundly. He backed off some distance and sat on the stump of the fallen tree, watching her with a sly gleam in his eye which was disturbingly familiar. Tess picked up the ring and marched in through the tunnel entrance, then went into the deepest corner of the bramble patch and dropped it there behind a big stone. But when she turned round, she found the chipmunk right behind her, watching every move she made. She sprang at him, chattering and scolding as loudly as she could, and he bolted away towards the light at the tunnel entrance.

# Acknowledgements

The publishers gratefully acknowledge permission to reproduce the following copyright material:

For the extract taken from *Aquila* Copyright © Andrew Norriss 1997, published by Penguin Books Ltd. For the extract taken from *Harry Potter and the Philosopher's Stone* published by Bloomsbury Publishing Plc, Copyright © J. K. Rowling 1997. For the extract taken from *Krindlekrax* Copyright © 1991 Philip Ridley, published by Jonathan Cape Ltd, a division of Random House UK Ltd. For the extract taken from *Matilda* Copyright © Roald Dahl Nominee Ltd 1988, published by Jonathan Cape Ltd, a division of Random House UK Ltd. For the extract taken from *Nightmare Stairs* Copyright © Robert Swindells 1997, published by Doubleday, a division of Transworld Publishers. All rights reserved. For the extract taken from *The Owl Tree* Copyright © Jenny Nimmo 1997. Illustrated by Anthony Lewis, reproduced by permission of the publisher, Walker Books Ltd, London. For the extract taken from *Pongwiffy and the Holiday of Doom* Copyright © Kaye Umansky 1995, reproduced by permission of the publisher, Viking Books, a division of Penguin Books Ltd. For the extract taken from *Skellig* Copyright © David Almond 1998, published by Hodder Children's Books. For the extract taken from *Snatchers* Copyright © Helen Cresswell 1998, published by Hodder Children's Books. For the extract taken from *Switchers* Copyright © Kate Thompson 1997, reproduced by permission of The Bodley Head Children's Books, a division of Random House UK Ltd.